CAROL ROTH has always loved writing. Carol's many wonderful books include *Five Little Ducklings Go to Bed*, *Where's My Mommy?*, *The Little School Bus*, *Who Will Tuck Me in Tonight?*, and *Ten Dirty Pigs/Ten Clean Pigs: An Upside-Down Turn-Around, Bath Time Counting Book*. Her books have won a Children's Choice Book Award (2005), the Missouri Building Block Award for Best Picture Book (2003), and the Parent's Guide to Children's Media Award for Outstanding Achievement in Children's Books (1999). Carol lives in New Jersey (USA) with her husband, Mark.

SEAN JULIAN enjoyed art from an early age, focusing on potato printmaking and creating plasticine dinosaurs. He now focuses his talents on children's book illustrations, where he can follow his passion to draw hairy gorillas, bears, and dinosaurs. His pictures delight and entertain. He lives in Bristol (UK).

To my mom, Jeanette, I will always love you.–C.R.

First published in the United States, Great Britain, Canada, Australia, and New Zealand in 2015 by NorthSouth Books, Inc., an imprint of NordSüd Verlag AG, CH-8050 Zürich, Switzerland.
First paperback edition 2019.

Distributed in the United States by NorthSouth Books, Inc., New York 10016.
Library of Congress Cataloging-in-Publication Data is available.
ISBN: 978-0-7358-4132-1 (trade edition)
ISBN: 978-0-7358-4346-2 (paperback edition)
1 3 5 7 9 • 10 8 6 4 2
Printed in China
www.northsouth.com

Carol Roth · Sean Julian

Five Little Ducklings
Go to School

North
South

Mama duck said, "Wake up. my dears.
Your first day of school is finally here!"

"YIPPEE! HOORAY! OH BOY! THAT'S COOL!"
Four little ducklings couldn't wait for school!

But the fifth little duckling sobbed, "BOO-HOO!
I won't go to school! I'm going to miss you!"

Then the fourth little ducking started to cry,
And the third little duckling had tears in his eyes!

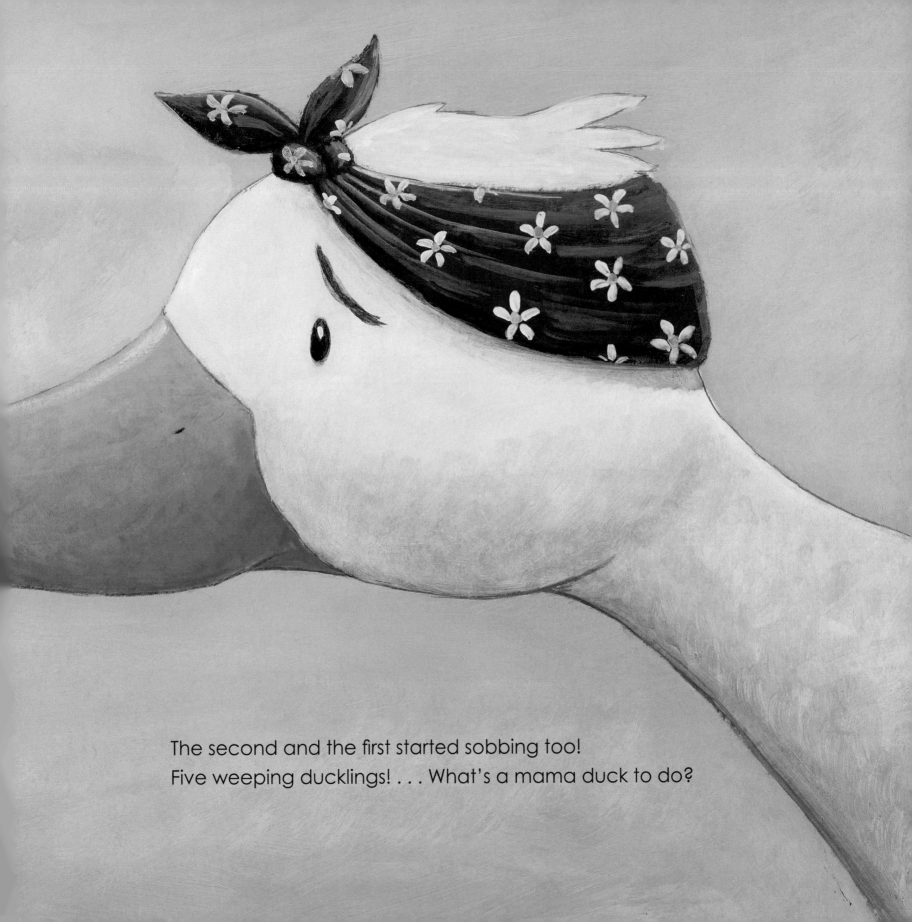

The second and the first started sobbing too!
Five weeping ducklings! . . . What's a mama duck to do?

"It's okay, little darlings," mama duck said.
And she kissed them all on the top of their heads.

Then mama duck told them, "Don't you cry.
I know it's hard to say good-bye.

"Don't be sad; don't be blue.
Teacher will take good care of you.

"Remember, my darlings, it's okay
To miss someone while they're away.

"Even though we'll be apart,
"We'll still be in each other's heart."

So five little ducklings wiped their eyes,
Waddled off to school with their heads held high.

Five little ducklings had lots of fun.
They played and laughed with everyone.

They drove the trucks and choo-choo trains,
Did some puzzles, played some games.

They painted pictures with red and blue,
Orange and yellow and purple too!

They built a tower oh so high,
So high it almost reached the sky!

What fun to be on the slide and swings

And play in the sandbox . . . so many fun things!

Story time was truly the best,
Snuggling together to read and rest.

And when the school day came to an end,
Mama duck said, "Did you make new friends?"

"Yes!" they shouted. "School's great, it's true.
We had so much fun . . . even though we missed you."

Five little ducklings hugged their mother,
Then five little ducklings hugged each other.

Five little ducklings all in a line
Waddled on home, feeling oh so fine.